SCOTT COUNTY LIBRARY
SHAKOPEE, MN 55379

CLEMSON TIGERS

BY TONY LEE

Published by ABDO Publishing Company, PO Box 398166, Minneapolis, MN 55439. Copyright © 2013 by Abdo Consulting Group, Inc. International copyrights reserved in all countries. No part of this book may be reproduced in any form without written permission from the publisher. SportsZone™ is a trademark and logo of ABDO Publishing Company.

Printed in the United States of America,
North Mankato, Minnesota
102012
012013

 THIS BOOK CONTAINS AT LEAST 10% RECYCLED MATERIALS.

Editor: Chrös McDougall
Series Designer: Craig Hinton

Photo Credits: Richard Shiro/AP Images, Cover; AP Images, Title, 25, 33; Jake Drake/AP Images, 4, 7, 11, 18, 42 (bottom left), 43 (top left); John Bazemore/AP Images, 8, 43 (bottom); Martin Fox/Getty Images, 12; Charles Rex Arbogast/AP Images, 17, 42 (top); Anderson Independent-Mail/Mark Crammer/AP Images, 21, 43 (top right); JPK/AP Images, 23; Clemson SID, 26; Richard Shiro/AP Images, 28, 42 (bottom right); Collegiate Images/AP Images, 31; Jerry Wachter/Getty Images, 34; Phil Coale/AP Images, 37; Craig Jones/Getty Images, 39; Jim R. Bounds/AP Images, 41; Simon Bruty /Sports Illustrated/Getty Images, 44

Cataloging-in-Publication Data
Lee, Tony.
 Clemson Tigers / Tony Lee.
   p. cm. -- (Inside college football)
Includes bibliographical references and index.
ISBN 978-1-61783-652-7
1. Clemson Tigers (Football team)--History--Juvenile literature. 2. Clemson University--Football--History--Juvenile literature. I. Title.
796.332--dc15

2012945886

TABLE OF CONTENTS

1. BACK ATOP THE ACC 5
2. HIGHS AND LOWS 13
3. HOWARD'S TIGERS 19
4. END OF AN ERA 27
5. CHAMPIONSHIP GLORY 35

TIMELINE 42
QUICK STATS 44
QUOTES & ANECDOTES 45
GLOSSARY 46
FOR MORE INFORMATION 47
INDEX 48
ABOUT THE AUTHOR 48

Clemson's Mike Bellamy runs the ball against Boston College during a 2011 game at Memorial Stadium.

BACK ATOP THE ACC

CLEMSON UNIVERSITY HAS BEEN A MEMBER OF THE ATLANTIC COAST CONFERENCE (ACC) SINCE 1953—THE YEAR THE LEAGUE WAS FORMED. THE TIGERS HAVE HAD PLENTY OF SUCCESS IN THE CONFERENCE. BUT ENTERING THE 2011 SEASON, THE TEAM HAD NOT WON AN ACC TITLE IN 20 YEARS.

Six other teams had won league championships in that time. Florida State had done it 12 times. Virginia Tech had done it four times. Meanwhile, the Tigers had been through many ups and downs.

The 2011 Clemson team was different, though. The school from the western part of South Carolina had talent on both sides of the football. The Tigers were especially good on offense. And things really came together in coach Dabo Swinney's third full season.

Clemson started the season with two easy wins. But its breakthrough came in the third game. The Auburn Tigers had

TIGERS

THE STREAK

Clemson started the 2011 season 2–0. But the wins were against Troy and Wofford, which were not strong teams. The Tigers were unranked. In fact, they received zero votes in the AP Poll that week.

That meant little on September 17, though. Auburn rolled into town and came face-to-face with one of college football's great pregame traditions. Clemson's players were dressed head to toe in orange. They surrounded Howard's Rock in the east end of Memorial Stadium. Then each of them raced from the rock to the field in the famous "Run down the Hill."

The Tigers continued running in the game. They gained 624 total yards. Tajh Boyd completed 30 passes for 386 yards. And the 38–24 win launched Clemson into the AP Poll's top 25. Then the Tigers beat Florida State and Virginia Tech in the next two weeks. That made Clemson the first ACC team to beat three straight ranked opponents.

won the 2010 national championship. They came to Clemson ranked twenty-first in the Associated Press (AP) Poll and with a 17-game winning streak. But the Tigers won 38–24.

Soon Clemson was 8–0. The Tigers jumped to sixth in the nation in the AP Poll. But then they began to struggle. They lost three of their final four regular-season games. Clemson sophomore quarterback Tajh Boyd threw seven interceptions in those four games. Among them was a loss to the rival South Carolina Gamecocks. The two in-state rivals had played each other every year since 1909.

The Tigers still finished the season 9–3. That was enough to win the ACC Atlantic Division and send them to the ACC Championship Game. But the Tigers' chances did not look good against the fifth-ranked Virginia Tech Hokies. Clemson had slipped back to twenty-first in the AP Poll. Plus, the Hokies were highly motivated. They had

Clemson's Andre Ellington breaks off a run during a 35–27 win over Wofford in 2011.

lost at home by 20 points to Clemson earlier in the year. Then they won seven straight games going into the ACC Championship Game.

The Hokies had the momentum. They had the high national ranking. And they had the recent success. But as it turned out, the Tigers wanted it more. Their program needed a big moment after years of waiting. There was hunger in that Clemson locker room.

The score was tied 10–10 at halftime. Then Clemson forced a punt to start the second half. That is when Boyd took over. He completed two big passes to sophomore wide receiver DeAndre Hopkins. Boyd ran

Clemson wide receiver Sammy Watkins breaks free from a Georgia Tech defender during a 2011 game in Atlanta.

twice for a total of 15 yards. Then Boyd hit junior tight end Dwayne Allen for an eight-yard touchdown.

　　The biggest play of the game came a few minutes later. Clemson had a first down on its own 47-yard line. Boyd took the snap and faked a handoff. He then rolled right into open field. He pumped once to fake a throw into the flat. And then he threw a bomb to Sammy Watkins. The freshman wide receiver caught the ball at the 10-yard line. He pulled a tricky stop-and-go move to get around the defense. Then he ran the ball into the end zone to complete a 53-yard scoring strike.

Clemson struck again less than two minutes later. Junior running back Andre Ellington ran the ball 29 yards for another touchdown. In a flash, the Tigers had built a 21-point lead.

Boyd scored another touchdown on a quarterback sneak early in the fourth quarter. The rout was on. The Tigers scored 28 straight points in less than 12 minutes. The feat was made even more impressive coming against the Hokies. They had one of the best defenses in the country.

YOUNG AND TALENTED

Clemson had a strong offense in 2011. It finished among the top 26 in yards and points per game. The Tigers were also very young. Sophomore quarterback Tajh Boyd led the ACC in completed passes, yards, and touchdowns. Freshman wide receiver Sammy Watkins was second in the league in receiving yards and tied for first in touchdowns. Sophomore wide receiver DeAndre Hopkins was right behind him on the leaderboards. And freshman running back Mike Bellamy averaged 6.0 yards per carry. Even sophomore kicker Chandler Catanzaro led the league in points and in field-goal percentage.

With a 38–10 win, Clemson once again was the king of the ACC. The Tigers had won 10 games for the first time since 1990. And they were headed to the Orange Bowl for the first time since 1981. Clemson had won the national championship that year. The Tigers would not be playing for a national title this time around. But going to the

Orange Bowl is a major achievement. The Orange Bowl is one of the premier bowls and is part of the Bowl Championship Series (BCS). It was especially important to Clemson fans. They had been waiting for years for this breakout 2011 season.

"There have been a lot of walls built up around this program over the last 20 years, and we knocked them down tonight," Swinney said. "We've been down in the valley, and the players locked arms and they charged up that hill."

IN MEMORY OF CHESTER

The Clemson community got sad news just before the 2011 ACC title game. Former Tigers defensive lineman Chester McGlockton had passed away at the age of 42. McGlockton had been an all-ACC performer. In 2011, he still ranked among the school's all-time leaders in sacks. He was a star when the team last won an ACC title in 1991. "I thought it was ironic that he was No. 91 and we won our first championship since '91," Clemson coach Dabo Swinney said after the win over Virginia Tech. "I'm happy how our players honored him tonight."

Boyd was named the ACC Championship Game's Most Valuable Player (MVP). He went 20-for-29 for 240 yards and three touchdown passes. He also gained 28 yards on the ground. Swinney said he would not trade any player in the country for his star quarterback. Boyd showed his maturity. He felt as if he and the program had turned a corner.

Clemson quarterback Tajh Boyd looks to pass during a 2011 game against Boston College.

"You get a sense of complacency if you let the outside world affect you," Boyd said in reference to the team's late-season slump. "That is one of the life lessons you learn. That's what happened. But it happened for a reason."

The season ended on a sour note. West Virginia clobbered Clemson 70–33 in the Orange Bowl, continuing the roller-coaster ride. But the 2011 season appeared to be the beginning of a new era. The Tigers had gone 10–4. And they had won a conference title. Now they were ready to take the next step.

Clemson College opened in 1893. The football team began playing three years later, in 1896.

HIGHS AND LOWS

RESIDENTS IN WESTERN SOUTH CAROLINA LOVE THEIR CLEMSON TIGERS. THAT WAS OBVIOUS FROM THE VERY START. THEY DID ALL THEY COULD TO BUILD A FOOTBALL PROGRAM THAT QUICKLY BECAME A POWER IN THE SOUTH.

Clemson College was founded in 1893. The football team began just three years later. Walter Riggs is considered to be the father of Clemson football. He was a professor at the school and also the first football coach. At the time, Riggs was one of only two people on campus who had ever seen a football game. After all, it was still a young sport.

Thirty students tried out for that first team. Twenty-one made it. The team won two of its three games that season. College football was still a bit different back then. The game play more resembled rugby than modern football. The massive stadiums and bright lights were still years away as well. Riggs came and went as coach in the early years.

THE INNOVATOR

John Heisman revolutionized offensive play. He is credited with inventing the center snap and the word "hike." He pioneered the forward pass and the handoff. The flea flicker and hidden ball trick also were Heisman's ideas.

Heisman liked to trick opponents off the field, as well. One legendary tale came from 1902. His Clemson team traveled to Atlanta to play Georgia Tech. The day before the game, Heisman sent a group of cadets to Atlanta to pose as Tigers players. He told them to party into the late hours. And he said to make sure Georgia Tech officials saw them doing it. Before long, the Yellow Jackets players got word of the late-night partying. They were sure they would have no problem winning the game. But Heisman had his real team stay in a quiet town up the road. The Tigers were rested and ready. And they destroyed Georgia Tech 44–5.

Before the 1900 season, he decided to focus strictly on his academic career.

So the Clemson College Athletic Association set out to find a new coach. Somebody recommended that the school hire up-and-coming coach John Heisman. Nobody knew it at the time, but his name would become the most famous in college football history. Since 1935, the Heisman Trophy has been given out to the best college football player each season.

Heisman coached at Clemson for just four years, from 1900 to 1903. But he had a tremendous impact. The Tigers went 6–0 in 1900 and outscored opponents 222–10.

The coach was a taskmaster. He disciplined his players. He always made sure they were in good shape. And he wanted his players to know original plays. Offenses were very basic at the time. So Heisman tried to set Clemson apart.

"At Clemson we have a style of football play radically different from any other on Earth," Heisman said. "Its notoriety and the fear and admiration of it have spread throughout the length and breadth of the entire southern world of football and further."

Clemson won the Southern Intercollegiate Athletic Association (SIAA) in Heisman's first year. Clemson then tied Cumberland 11–11 three years later in the SIAA title game. That was considered the school's first postseason game. Some called it the "Championship of the South."

That tie put the finishing touches on Heisman's 19–3–2 record at Clemson. He left for Georgia Tech after that. Clemson soon entered what has been called the "Dark Ages." From 1908 to 1926, the Tigers went 69–82–10 under nine different head coaches. The school left the SIAA for the Southern Conference in 1921. Among its 14 teams were Alabama, South Carolina, Georgia, Georgia Tech, and Auburn. But the losing continued for Clemson.

"BIG THURSDAY"

Clemson and South Carolina first met on November 12, 1896, at the State Fair in Columbia, South Carolina. The Gamecocks won that first game 12–6. The game was then cancelled in 1901. And the rivalry was suspended from 1903 to 1908 after a near-brawl between students from both schools. But in every other year from 1896 to 1959, the game was played on Thursday at the State Fair. That is how it came to be called "Big Thursday." Since 1960, the game has alternated between Clemson and Columbia on a yearly basis.

The turnaround finally came when Josh Cody took over as coach in 1927. He led the Tigers to a 5–3–1 record in his first year. Then he guided the team to three straight eight-win seasons. The 1928 team was famous for being the first Clemson squad to wear bright orange uniforms. Today, Clemson is known for them.

Cody resigned after the 1930 season. He had a 29–11–1 record at Clemson. But fans remembered him most for beating South Carolina in all four seasons.

It was hard to win in the powerful Southern Conference. Financial issues at Clemson made it even tougher. Jess Neely took over for Cody. The Tigers struggled in his first three seasons. Then he was able to convince the school to put more money into the program. If Clemson was to be a college football force, he said it would need better locker rooms, new equipment, and facilities that would attract the best players.

Neely slowly began to reestablish the program. The team went just 24–32–5 from when Neely took over in 1930 through the first four weeks of the 1937 season. Then Clemson beat South Carolina. Neely went 18–3–2 in his career at Clemson after that. And in 1939, Clemson football once again became a force.

The 1939 season began with a win over Presbyterian. Then Clemson lost by one point to Tulane. But the Tigers did not lose again. They shut out South Carolina 27–0. They defeated Wake Forest 20–7. And they beat Southern Conference foe Furman 14–3. Clemson held every opponent to single digits.

> The Heisman Trophy, named after former Clemson coach John Heisman, is given to college football's best player each season.

That was the first Clemson team to be ranked since the AP Poll began in 1936. It also was the first to play in a bowl game. The fifteenth-ranked Tigers played the fourteenth-ranked Boston College Eagles in the Cotton Bowl. All-American running back Banks McFadden led Clemson into the game in Dallas. The Tigers outlasted Boston College by a 6–3 score in front of 20,000 fans. Clemson running back Charlie Timmons scored the winning touchdown in the second quarter.

Just a few weeks later, Neely left Clemson to take a job at Rice. This time, however, the coaching transition was smoother. Frank Howard, an assistant under Neely since 1931, was ready to take over.

Clemson's mascot, the Tiger, was introduced in 1954 when a student first dressed up as a tiger.

3

HOWARD'S TIGERS

EVERY MAJOR COLLEGE FOOTBALL PROGRAM HAD TO TAKE A BIG STEP FORWARD AT SOME POINT. FOR CLEMSON, THAT STEP CAME DURING THE EARLY 1940S.

Frank Howard took over as coach for Jess Neely after the Cotton Bowl win on January 1, 1940. Howard had been Neely's assistant, and he kept the same system in place. But he had a different style. It fit perfectly. Howard remained the guiding force behind Clemson football for the next three decades.

Howard led the Tigers to a Southern Conference title in his very first year. He went 13–4–1 in his first two years. Clemson was nationally ranked both seasons. Before his third year, the program continued to grow. Construction of Memorial Stadium had begun.

There was a lot of excitement when the new stadium opened in 1942. However, football took a back seat for a few

TIGERS

HOME SWEET HOME

When Jess Neely became Clemson coach in 1931, he took over a winning program. But the facilities and equipment were old and run down. Even fan interest was low at the time. Neely wanted improvements to help his team compete for conference titles. Yet he thought building a new stadium was a waste of time.

"Don't ever let them talk you into building a big stadium," Neely said as he left for Rice. "Put about 10,000 seats behind the YMCA. That's all you'll ever need."

But Clemson did build a new stadium. There were roughly 20,000 seats when Memorial Stadium opened on September 19, 1942. More than 60,000 seats have been added since then. Entering the 2011 season, Memorial Stadium was the seventeenth-largest campus stadium in the country. Officially, it has 81,500 seats but has squeezed in many more fans for big games.

years after it was built. The United States was in World War II from 1941 to 1945. Many young men who might otherwise be going to college were sent off to fight. That had an effect on college and professional sports teams around the country, including Clemson. The Tigers had three straight losing seasons before going 6–3–1 in 1945.

Things finally came back together for Clemson in 1948. Many remember it as the first great season in Clemson football history.

The season started with a 53–0 rout of Presbyterian. Then the Tigers beat North Carolina State and Mississippi State. After that was one of the more famous games in the rivalry with South Carolina.

The Gamecocks had a 7–6 lead late in the game. They tried to pin the Tigers deep with a punt. But Clemson senior tackle and co-captain Phil Prince broke through South Carolina's offensive line and got his hands on the kick. The ball

Memorial Stadium, which is nicknamed "Death Valley," was built in 1942 and now seats 81,500 fans.

squirted away before Clemson defensive end Oscar Thompson scooped it up and ran into the end zone. The final score was 13–7. The Tigers had survived.

In fact, they found a way to survive many times that year. Clemson ended up going 11–0 that season. That included a one-point win over the Missouri Tigers in the Gator Bowl. The Clemson Tigers were a scrappy bunch who won six games by seven points or less.

"It was a very quick team, but mainly, a bunch of players who gave their all," Prince said. "And the thing that amazes me is that this was the same team that was a losing team in 1947. Everybody on that team was very close to everybody else."

At the time, Howard called his undefeated crew "the best team I have ever coached."

That also was the year that Memorial Stadium became known as a more intimidating place. Clemson annually opened the season against Presbyterian at the time. The Tigers had won the last four games by a combined score of 191–0, all at home. The 1948 game was at Clemson as well.

When speaking with reporters about the upcoming game, Presbyterian coach Lonnie McMillian called the stadium "Death Valley." The nickname stuck. And as Clemson piled up home wins over the years, the name took on a whole new meaning.

That 1948 team established Clemson as a national power. Howard led the Tigers to another undefeated season in 1950. That team

A ONE-SIDED RIVALRY

The Clemson and Presbyterian football teams met at Clemson to start the season every year from 1930 to 1957. Presbyterian coach Lonnie McMillian feared Memorial Stadium, and he had a good reason for it. He coached his team at "Death Valley" 13 times from 1941 to 1953. In the final 10 visits, his team was outscored 507–33. However, there was one trip that went right for McMillian. In 1943, Presbyterian defeated the Tigers 13–12 in Memorial Stadium.

Clemson tailback Billy Hair runs around Miami defenders during the Gator Bowl following the 1951 season.

went 9–0–1. The tie came against South Carolina. Clemson beat all of its other regular-season opponents by an average of more than 33 points.

The Tigers earned a berth in the Orange Bowl that year against the Miami Hurricanes. The Orange Bowl was held in Miami's home stadium. Many people in the southern part of Florida looked down on Clemson. They thought it was a lesser opponent. Howard disagreed.

"They ought to read the AP Poll if they want to know about Clemson," he said.

TIGERS

The Tigers were ranked eleventh in the nation. The Hurricanes were ranked fourteenth. Howard's team backed up its ranking with a 15–14 win. However, the victory came in an odd way. Miami had the ball with a 14–13 lead in the fourth quarter. The Hurricanes then had a punt return for a touchdown called back because of multiple penalties. Now they were backed up to their own 1-yard line. Moments later, Clemson guard Sterling Smith broke through the Miami line. He tackled Hurricanes running back Frank Smith in the end zone for a go-ahead safety.

Neely had moved the football program ahead with the eight-win seasons and the Cotton Bowl win after the 1939 season. That dramatic victory in the Orange Bowl after the 1950 season helped Clemson take another step forward. It also began the most successful decade in Tigers history up to that point.

Clemson appeared in the Gator Bowl after the 1951 season, the Orange Bowl after the 1956 season, and the Sugar Bowl after the

STREAKING TIGERS

Frank Howard's teams in the late part of the 1940s were very good. At times, they were unbeatable. From November 8, 1947, through September 17, 1949, they went 15–0. Through 2011, that remained the longest winning streak in program history. However, the Tigers actually had 16 straight weeks without a loss. Beginning with the final three games of the 1949 season and extending into the early part of the 1951 season, they were 14–0–2.

> Clemson fullback Doug Cline fumbles as he runs against Texas Christian University in the 1959 Bluebonnet Bowl in Houston.

1958 season. The Tigers were league champions in each of the latter two seasons. Clemson finished the decade with a 9–2 season and a win in the Bluebonnet Bowl in 1959.

The school had competed as an independent for one year, in 1952. Then Clemson became a charter member of the ACC in 1953. There were six other teams in the league that year. Virginia joined the following year to make it an eight-team conference. It would remain that way for nearly two decades.

Clemson coach Frank Howard led the Tigers to a 165–118–12 record from 1940 to 1969.

END OF AN ERA

THE 1960S WERE AN ODD TIME FOR CLEMSON FOOTBALL. THE TIGERS ENDED THE 1950S BY GOING TO THREE BOWL GAMES IN FOUR YEARS. THEN THEY BEGAN 1960 AS THE NINTH-RANKED TEAM IN THE COUNTRY. A 3–0 START BOOSTED THAT RANKING TO NUMBER SEVEN.

However, a loss at Maryland on October 15, 1960, seemed to start a decline. From that point until the end of the decade, Clemson was 47–48–2. And the team never won more than six games or went to a bowl game. But there was one positive. The league was not very strong at the time. So the Tigers still won ACC titles in 1965, 1966, and 1967.

The program continued to take shape in other ways under Frank Howard. While the Tigers were battling for ACC titles in the middle of the decade, they also were establishing traditions that would become famous throughout college football.

Touching Howard's Rock before a home game remains one of the honored traditions for Clemson players.

Originally, the team dressed for games at Fike Fieldhouse and then walked to nearby Memorial Stadium. The players entered under a scoreboard in the east end zone. From there, they jogged down a hill and onto the field for their warm-ups.

For years, there was nothing more to it. It was just how they entered the stadium and got ready to play. But one day a fan gave Howard a rock that was about the size of a football. Howard placed that rock atop the hill in 1966. Soon players began to rub the rock and then dash to the field. The "Run Down the Hill" was first done in 1967 before a win over Wake Forest. Howard used it to motivate his players.

"If you're going to give me 110 percent, you can rub that rock," he told them. "If you're not, keep your filthy hands off it."

The rock became known as Howard's Rock. It paired perfectly with the dash to the field. And a tradition was born.

Between the Death Valley nickname, Howard's Rock, and the "Run Down the Hill," Clemson home games had become something special. During Howard's time as coach, the team went undefeated at home 10 times. That only added to the mystique.

The Howard era ended after the 1969 team went 4–6. It was the team's second straight losing season. Three more losing seasons came under new coach Hootie Ingram and another followed under Red Parker. Parker had a 7–4 season in 1974 but was fired after going 2–9 and 3–6–2 in the next two seasons. The program had gone 18 years without a bowl game or a national ranking. The Tigers were in a slump.

HOOTIE'S WAY

Taking over for Frank Howard was not an easy thing to do. Hootie Ingram not only had a 12–21 record in his three years as head coach, but he also nearly put an end to the "Run Down the Hill." In 1970 and 1971, Ingram had the team instead dress in the west end and make its entrance there.

The Tigers were 6–9 at home under Ingram. Then they decided to mix things up before a game with South Carolina to close out the 1972 season. They rubbed the rock, ran down the hill, and survived a memorable 7–6 win over their bitter rivals. The team has entered the field of play by rubbing Howard's Rock and racing down the hill ever since.

TIGERS

Still, there were some quality players in the program when Charley Pell took over as coach in 1977. Among them was quarterback Steve Fuller. He would blossom under Pell.

Fuller had started nine games for the 1976 team. In 1977, he won the first of two straight ACC Player of the Year Awards. That season, Fuller led the Tigers to an 8–3–1 record and a berth in the Gator Bowl. Pittsburgh crushed Clemson in the bowl game. But at least the Tigers were back on the map.

One of the most famous plays in Clemson-South Carolina history came that season. With his team trailing, Fuller hit junior wide receiver Jerry Butler for a last-minute touchdown to claim the win. The twisting 20-yard grab at the goal line ended a dramatic game in dramatic fashion.

FULLER AND COMPANY

Quarterback Steve Fuller was one of four Clemson players to achieve All-America status between 1977 and 1979. Offensive lineman Joe Bostic was an All-American in 1977 and 1978. He later played 10 years in the National Football League (NFL). Wide receiver Jerry Butler made the All-America team in 1978. He was Fuller's favorite target. Defensive tackle Jim Stuckey was honored in 1979 when he had 10 sacks.

Fuller was a senior in 1978. In the Tigers' second game of the season, Georgia shut out Clemson 12–0. But Clemson came roaring back. It averaged 32.6 points per game in winning its next nine games. Soon the Tigers were back in the Gator Bowl. Only this time, it was

Clemson's Perry Tuttle runs the ball against South Carolina. Tuttle played at Clemson from 1978 to 1981.

under different circumstances. Pell had a job locked up with Florida starting after the season. So he did not coach in the bowl game against Ohio State.

Pell recommended assistant head coach Danny Ford as a replacement. So Ford took over before the Gator Bowl. But at 30, Ford was the youngest head coach in Division I football. And his first game was against legendary Ohio State coach Woody Hayes.

The Tigers pulled off the upset. However, the game is most remembered for one wild moment in the fourth quarter. Ohio State trailed 17–15 with two minutes remaining. But the Buckeyes were driving down the field. Then Clemson linebacker Charlie Bauman ended their hopes by intercepting a pass.

On the return, Bauman was knocked out of bounds near Hayes. The Buckeyes' coach then punched Bauman. Hayes had to be restrained by his own players to prevent him from again hitting Bauman. A brawl broke out. Hayes was penalized twice and the game soon ended. Even a year later, Bauman still was answering questions about the incident.

"I don't like to talk about it," he said in 1979. "Why? Because right now I'm known as the guy Woody Hayes hit. I'm a football player, and I'd like to be known as a football player."

Regardless of how it ended, Ford had defeated a legend. After eight losing seasons in nine years, Clemson was among the country's top

WOODY

Legendary Ohio State coach Woody Hayes was fired the morning after he punched Clemson linebacker Charlie Bauman. Hayes finished his coaching career with 238 wins—205 of them at Ohio State. Hayes never apologized to Bauman. However, he did call Bauman a few months later and congratulated him on the victory.

> Ohio State coach Woody Hayes is seen punching Clemson's Charlie Bauman at the Gator Bowl in 1978.

programs. It was ranked sixth in the nation when the final AP Poll came out that year. That was the highest ranking in team history.

With an enthusiastic young coach and many talented players, the future looked bright for Clemson. Ford's first full season in 1979 resulted in an 8–4 record. The Tigers also were invited to the Peach Bowl, where they lost to Baylor.

Despite the loss, the Tigers could still be proud. They had reached a bowl game in three consecutive years for the first time in school history. And the seniors on that 1979 team had won a school record 27 games. The 1980s had the potential to be a special time in Clemson, South Carolina.

END OF AN ERA

Maryland needed two players to try to stop Clemson defensive lineman William "The Refrigerator" Perry in 1981.

CHAMPIONSHIP GLORY

IN 1980, CLEMSON FINISHED THE SEASON JUST 6–5. THE TIGERS CAME INTO THE 1981 SEASON UNRANKED. COACH DANNY FORD WAS EXCITED ABOUT HIS TEAM'S CHANCES, THOUGH.

Ford had many players returning. Some of the players had been around during the stretch of three straight bowl games at the end of the 1970s. Among them were senior linebacker Jeff Davis, senior wide receiver Perry Tuttle, and standout junior defensive back Terry Kinard. Meanwhile, freshman defensive lineman William "The Refrigerator" Perry was proving to be a force as well.

Those players helped form a unit that had talent on both sides of the ball. The defense was particularly good. It held the team's first seven opponents to 10 points or less.

The offense really shined against Wake Forest in the eighth game of the season. The Tigers set an ACC record for points (82) and a school record for yards (756) in the

TIGERS

STAR POWER

Jeff Davis, Perry Tuttle, and Terry Kinard were three of five All-Americans on the 1981 roster. Senior defensive tackle Jeff Bryant and senior offensive tackle Lee Nanney were the others. That team had 23 players who would be all-ACC selections at some point in their careers. A total of 31 players on that championship squad eventually were drafted into the NFL.

Davis and Kinard are two of the three Clemson players in the College Football Hall of Fame. Banks McFadden, the 1939 football and basketball All-American, is the other. Davis is thought of as one of the great leaders in program history. He had 175 tackles in 1981. In a 1980 game against North Carolina, he recorded an amazing 24 tackles. That was the second-most in a single game in Tigers history. Meanwhile, Kinard finished his career with a school-record 17 interceptions.

82–24 win. Clemson followed up that performance with a much closer win at eighth-ranked North Carolina. Then the Tigers got past Maryland and South Carolina.

Clemson was 11–0 and ranked first in the nation. It only needed to get past Nebraska in the Orange Bowl and the unthinkable would happen—Clemson would be the national champion.

The punishing defense let the high-powered Cornhuskers know they were in for a battle. Nebraska went three and out on eight of its 12 possessions. It pulled to within 22–15 late in the fourth quarter. But the Tigers drained most of the remaining clock to seal the win. Clemson junior quarterback Homer Jordan was the MVP. He threw for one touchdown to Tuttle and also ran for 46 yards. That included a 23-yard run to pick up a huge first down with about two minutes remaining. And to think, the team almost moved him to defense before his sophomore year.

> Clemson fullback Tracy Johnson flips over the Stanford line in search of the end zone during the 1986 Gator Bowl.

Ford was happy to let the rest of the country know a little more about Clemson football.

"We finally proved that there's more to the ACC than basketball," he said. "They didn't believe [in] this team in Las Vegas [where betting odds were made]. Nebraska was favored. They didn't believe [in] this team in Nebraska. Out there the newspapers were asking if we belonged in the big time. Well, you can't brag until you've proved your facts. We've proved it. Now, we can brag."

They could continue to brag for the next couple of years. The Tigers followed up the national title with back-to-back 9–1–1 seasons. They

TIGERS

> ### NCAA VIOLATIONS
>
> The National Collegiate Athletic Association (NCAA) found 150 rule violations at Clemson from 1977 to the early part of 1982. Clemson's program was placed on probation. The Tigers were banned from bowl games in 1982 and 1983 and barred from national television in 1983 and 1984. The NCAA also cut down on the number of scholarships that the school could give out to incoming players. The Tigers were allowed to keep their 1981 national title. The program was one of many powers to go on probation in a short span, including Georgia, Southern Methodist, and Arizona State.

were undefeated in the ACC both years. And the Ford era ended in 1989 after three straight 10-win seasons and four straight bowl wins.

The 1980s went down as perhaps the best decade in Clemson football history. The 1990s, however, were more difficult.

Ford resigned after the 1989 season due to rule violations. Ken Hatfield took Ford's place as coach. Hatfield led his first team in 1990 to a 10–2 record and a win in the Hall of Fame Bowl. It was the fifth straight bowl win for the program. But the rest of the decade included three losing seasons and one 6–6 year.

The 6–6 season was in 1999, the first under coach Tommy Bowden. He is the son of famed Florida State coach Bobby Bowden, and he had coached Tulane to an 11–0 record in 1998.

The Bowden name was well respected in college football. That is one reason why the first meeting between father and son on October 23, 1999, was such a big event. It was called the "Bowden Bowl." The attendance

Clemson quarterback Woodrow Dantzler passes against the Missouri Tigers during a 2000 game at Memorial Stadium.

of 86,092 still stood as a Memorial Stadium record in 2011. However, the father came out on top as Florida State won 17–14.

Tommy Bowden went 72–45 in nine-and-a-half seasons at Clemson. He never had a losing season, and he took Clemson to eight bowl games. However, Bowden never won the ACC, and some of his teams fell short of expectations. He resigned six games into the 2008 season. His team began the season ranked ninth in the nation but started just 3–3.

The 1980s had featured some of the program's best defensive players of all time. The Bowden era had produced some great offensive

CHAMPIONSHIP GLORY

BOWDEN BOWL

Tommy Bowden faced his father Bobby Bowden nine times from 1999 to 2007. In every one of those matchups, Bobby's Florida State Seminoles were a ranked team and Tommy's Clemson Tigers were an unranked team. Despite that, son Tommy got the better of his father four times in the Bowden Bowl. In 2003, Clemson defeated third-ranked Florida State 26–10 to give Tommy Bowden his first win over his father. Clemson also won the final three times they met.

stars. First on that list was quarterback Woodrow "Woody" Dantzler. Tommy West, the coach before Bowden, had recruited Dantzler. But Dantzler became a starter in Bowden's first year. He was instantly one of the more dynamic players in school history.

In 2001, Dantzler became the first player in college football history to pass for 2,000 yards and run for 1,000 yards in the same season. The year after he left, fans saw the debut of quarterback Charlie Whitehurst. He graduated after the 2005 season as the school leader in almost every major passing category.

A freshman running back named C. J. Spiller began to make some noise soon after. Spiller gained 1,148 yards from scrimmage and scored 12 touchdowns in his freshman year. By the time he left in 2009, Spiller had gained 7,588 all-purpose yards. That was the most in school history. His 21 touchdowns in 2009 were a school record, as were his 51 career touchdowns.

Clemson star running back C. J. Spiller runs away from North Carolina State defenders during a 2009 game.

One man who worked closely with Whitehurst and Spiller was Dabo Swinney. He was the wide receivers' coach from 2003 to 2006. Then he became the assistant head coach under Bowden in 2007 and 2008. When Bowden resigned under pressure, Swinney was selected to replace him. With a blend of youthful excitement and a love for high-powered offensive football, Swinney quickly had a major impact on the program.

In his three full seasons, the Tigers climbed back to the top of the ACC. With Swinney at the helm and a solid flow of talent making its way to Clemson, the program looked to be back among the nation's best.

TIMELINE

On October 31, Clemson plays its first football game. The team defeats Furman 14–6 in Greenville, South Carolina.

1896

On November 10, Clemson defeats rival South Carolina for the first time.

1897

John Heisman is named Clemson's head coach on December 8.

1899

Clemson joins the Southern Conference. It is one of 14 teams to make up the new league.

1921

Josh Cody takes over as Clemson's head coach.

1927

On December 4, the Tigers defeat Citadel to finish the regular season 10–0. They later defeat Missouri in the Gator Bowl to complete an undefeated season.

1948

On May 8, Clemson joins the ACC. Six other teams are part of the new league.

1953

Clemson wins its first ACC title and accepts an invitation for the Orange Bowl.

1956

On September 24, Howard's Rock makes its first appearance at Memorial Stadium.

1966

On December 10, Howard resigns as Clemson's head coach.

1969

The Tigers play with new uniforms featuring the brilliant orange for the first time.

On January 17, Jess Neely is named Clemson's head coach.

Clemson is ranked nationally for the first time. Banks McFadden is the team's first All-American. And the Tigers accept a bowl bid for the first time, defeating Boston College 6–3 in the Cotton Bowl on January 1, 1940.

On January 11, Frank Howard is named head coach at Clemson.

Memorial Stadium opens with a 32–13 win over Presbyterian.

1928 | **1931** | **1939** | **1940** | **1942**

On January 1, Clemson defeats Nebraska in the Orange Bowl to finish the season undefeated and win the national championship.

Clemson defeats South Carolina 45–0. It is the largest margin of victory in the rivalry in 89 years. That record would be broken in 2003, when the Tigers won 63–17.

On December 2, Tommy Bowden is named Clemson's head coach.

On October 14, Bowden resigns and Dabo Swinney is named Clemson's interim head coach. Swinney later takes over as head coach.

On December 3, Clemson defeats Virginia Tech for its first ACC title in 20 years.

1982 | **1989** | **1998** | **2008** | **2011**

QUICK STATS

PROGRAM INFO
Clemson College (1896–1963)
Clemson University Tigers (1964–)

NATIONAL CHAMPIONSHIP
1981

OTHER ACHIEVEMENTS
BCS bowl appearances (1999–): 1
Southern Conference
 championships (1921–52): 2
ACC championships (1953–): 14
Bowl record: 16–18

KEY PLAYERS
(POSITION[S]; SEASONS WITH TEAM)
Jerry Butler (WR; 1975–78)
Fred Cone (RB; 1948–50)
Jeff Davis (LB; 1978–81)
Steve Fuller (QB; 1975–78)
Terry Kinard (DB; 1979–82)
Banks McFadden (HB; 1937–39)
Michael Dean Perry (DT; 1984–87)
William Perry (DT; 1981–84)
C. J. Spiller (RB; 2006–09)

KEY COACHES
Danny Ford (1978–89):
 96–29–4; 6–2 (bowl games)
Frank Howard (1940–69):
 165–118–12; 3–3 (bowl games)
Jess Neely (1931–39):
 43–35–7; 1–0 (bowl games)

HOME STADIUM
Clemson Memorial Stadium (1942–)

* All statistics through 2011 season

QUOTES & ANECDOTES

"This is a game that's not always won by the best football team or by who's supposed to be the best football team. But on that Saturday, you prove who has the best football team. Now, Alabama-Auburn is a great, great rivalry, and they get after it. They have their land-grant jokes; and there's books of 100 Alabama jokes and 100 Auburn jokes—just like it is here. But they let it die about the end of February. The Clemson-South Carolina rivalry, they don't let it die. For 365 days a year there's somebody at every function you go to who's talking about Clemson or South Carolina against each other. It's simply the biggest and best rivalry in football." —Clemson coach Danny Ford on the rivalry with South Carolina

Among the many changes John Heisman brought to the Clemson program was his opinion on drinking and eating. He wanted his players to avoid anything with hot water, from coffee to soup, thinking that it weakened people. Heisman banned many other foods, as well, but urged his players to eat raw meat.

William "The Refrigerator" Perry became famous after he entered the NFL. As a rookie, he was a key member of the Chicago Bears' dominant defense in 1985. At 335 pounds, he also was used as a blocking back near the goal line and even scored a touchdown in the Super Bowl that season. Perry once was asked what his biggest weakness was. He replied, "Cheeseburgers."

GLOSSARY

All-American
Players chosen as one of the best amateurs in the country in a particular activity.

bowl game
A game after the season that teams earn the right to play in by having a good record.

conference
In sports, a group of teams that play each other each season.

draft
A system used by professional sports leagues to select new players in order to spread incoming talent among all teams. The NFL Draft is held each April.

momentum
A continued strong performance based on recent success.

ranking
A national position as determined by voters.

rival
An opponent that brings out great emotion in players and fans.

scholarship
Financial assistance awarded to students to help them pay for school.

upset
A game in which the team expected to lose emerges victorious.

FOR MORE INFORMATION

FURTHER READING

Bourret, Tim. *The Clemson University Football Vault: The History of the Tigers.* Florence, AL: Whitman Publishing, 2008.

Bradley, Bob. *Death Valley Days: The Glory of Clemson Football.* Athens, GA: Longstreet Press, 1991.

Haney, Travis, and Larry Williams. *Classic Clashes of the Carolina-Clemson Football Rivalry: A State of Disunion.* Charleston, SC: The History Press, 2011.

WEB LINKS

To learn more about the Clemson Tigers, visit ABDO Publishing Company online at **www.abdopublishing.com**. Web sites about the Tigers are featured on our Book Links page. These links are routinely monitored and updated to provide the most current information available.

PLACES TO VISIT

Clemson Memorial Stadium
Avenue of Champions
Clemson, South Carolina 29634
864-656-1935
www.clemsontigers.com/ViewArticle.dbml?DB_OEM_ID=28500&ATCLID=205504990

Built in 1942, this is the seventeenth-largest on-campus football stadium in the country. It was named to honor Clemson alumni who had died in service.

College Football Hall of Fame
111 South St. Joseph Street
South Bend, Indiana 46601
1-800-440-FAME (3263)
www.collegefootball.org

This hall of fame and museum highlights the greatest players and moments in the history of college football. Among the former Tigers enshrined here are Jeff Davis, Terry Kinard, Banks McFadden, and coach Frank Howard.

INDEX

Allen, Dwayne, 8

Bauman, Charlie, 32
Bellamy, Mike, 9
"Big Thursday," 15
Bostic, Joe, 30
Bowden, Tommy (coach), 38–41
Boyd, Tajh, 6, 7–8, 9, 10–11
Bryant, Jeff, 36
Butler, Jerry, 30

Catanzaro, Chandler, 9
Cody, Josh (coach), 16

Dantzler, Woodrow "Woody," 40
Davis, Jeff, 35, 36

Ellington, Andre, 9

Florida State, 5, 6, 38–39, 40
Ford, Danny (coach), 31–33, 35, 37–38
Fuller, Steve, 30

Georgia Tech, 14, 15

Hatfield, Ken (coach), 38
Heisman, John (coach), 14–15
Hopkins, DeAndre, 7, 9
Howard, Frank (coach), 17, 19, 22, 23, 24, 27–29
Howard's Rock, 6, 28–29

Ingram, Hootie (coach), 29

Jordan, Homer, 36

Kinard, Terry, 35, 36

Maryland, 27, 36
McFadden, Banks, 17, 36
McGlockton, Chester, 10
Memorial Stadium, 6, 19–20, 22, 28, 29, 39

Nanney, Lee, 36
Neely, Jess (coach), 16, 17, 19, 20, 24

Orange Bowl, 9–10, 11, 23–24, 36–37

Parker, Red (coach), 29
Pell, Charley (coach), 30, 31

Perry, William "The Refrigerator," 35
Prince, Phil, 20–22

Riggs, Walter (coach), 13
"Run down the Hill," 6, 28–29

Smith, Sterling, 24
South Carolina, 6, 15, 16, 20–21, 23, 29, 30, 33, 36
Spiller, C. J., 40–41
Stuckey, Jim, 30
Swinney, Dabo (coach), 5, 10, 41

Thompson, Oscar, 21
Timmons, Charlie, 17
Tuttle, Perry, 35, 36

Virginia Tech, 5, 6–7, 9, 10

Wake Forest, 16, 28, 35
Watkins, Sammy, 8, 9
West, Tommy (coach), 40
Whitehurst, Charlie, 40–41

ABOUT THE AUTHOR

Tony Lee is a sportswriter based in Boston. He completed his undergraduate studies at the University of Vermont and his graduate work at Emerson College. He served as a writer and editor at ESPN in Bristol, Connecticut, and later as the Boston Red Sox beat writer for the New England Sports Network. Lee has covered the Red Sox, the Celtics, and the Bruins for a variety of publications and Web sites, including ESPNBoston.com and the *Boston Metro*.